VENUS ENSLAVED

Venus Enslaved

by Manly Wade Wellman

What chance had the castaway Earthman and his crossbow-weaponed Amazons against the mighty Frogmasters of the Veiled Planet?

Black velvet infinity all around, punctured and patterned with the many-hued jewels of space—comforting, somehow, because they made the same constellation patterns you used to see on Earth. There was the Dipper, there Scorpio, there Orion. But the twinkle was shut off, as though every star had turned cold and silently watchful toward your impudent invasion of emptiness.

So big was the universe that the little recess which did duty for control-room, observation-point and living-cabin seemed even smaller than it was; which was very small indeed. Planter forgot the dizzy lightness of head and body, here beyond gravity, and turned his wondering eyes outward from where he lay strapped in his spring-jointed hammock, toward the firmament, and decided that there was nothing in all his past life that he would change if he could.

"Check blast-tempo," came the voice of Disbro just beyond his head, a high, harsh, commanding voice. "Check lubrication-loss and check sun-direction. Then brace yourself. We may land quicker than we thought."

Planter leaned toward the instrument panel that covered most of the bulkhead to the right of his hammock. The pale glow from the dials highlighted his face, young, bony, intent. "Blast-tempo adequate," he called back to Disbro. "Lubrication-loss about seven point two. Three point nine six degrees off sunward. Air loss nil."

"Who asked for air loss?" snubbed Disbro from his hammock forward. He was leaner than Planter, taller, older. Even in his insulated coveralls, bulking against whatever temperature or pressure danger might be threatened by the outer space, he was of a dangerous elegance of figure and attitude. His face, framed in tight, cushioned helmet, was so narrow that it seemed compressed sidewise—dark eyes crowded together with only a disdainful blade of nose between them, a mouth short but strong, a chin like the pointed toe of a stylish boot, a cropped black mustache. Back on lost Earth, Disbro had

5

frightened men and fascinated women. His cunning crime-administration had been almost too neat for the police, but not quite; or he would not have been here, with his life barely held in his elegant fingertips.

"Venus plumb center ahead," he told Planter. "Have a look."

That last as if he were granting a favor. Planter twisted in the hammock. He saw the taut-slung cocoon that would be Disbro's netted body, the control board like a bigger, more complex typewriter where Disbro could reach and strike key-combinations to steer, speed or otherwise maneuver the ship.

Beyond, a great round port, at its middle a disk the size of a table-top. Against the black, airless sky, most of that disk looked as blue as the thinnest of milk. One smooth edge was brightened to cream—the sunward limb of Venus. But even the dimmer expanse showed fluffy and gently rippling, a swaddling of opaque cloud.

"That," said Disbro, "is our little gray home in the west."

"I wonder what's underneath the clouds," mused Planter, for the millionth time.

"All those science-pots, sitting home on the seats of their expensive striped pants, wonder that," snarled Disbro. "That's why they sent eight rockets before us, smack into the cloud. That's why, with eight silences out of a possible eight, they rigged this ninth. That's why, when nobody was fool enough to volunteer, they dug up three convicts who were all neatly earmarked to be killed anyway, and gave them a bang at the job."

Three convicts—Planter, Disbro, and Max. Planter had forgotten Max, as everyone was apt to, including Max himself. For Max had been a sturdy athlete, a coming heavyweight champion, until too many gaily-accepted blows had done something to his mind. Doctors said some concussion unbalanced him, but not far enough so that he didn't know right and wrong apart when he killed his manager for cheating on certain gate receipts. And so, prison and a sentence to the chair with the reprieve that came by recommendation of the Rocket Foundation on March 30, 2082. Now Max was in the compartment aft, keeping the levers kicking that ran the rocket engines. Show Max how to do a thing and he'd keep right on doing it until you pulled him away, or until he dropped.

What would Max's last name be, wondered Planter. He studied the face of Venus. He sang to himself, softly:

"*Oh, thou sublime sweet evening star....*"

Softly, but not too softly for Disbro's excellent ears. Disbro chuckled.

"You know opera, Planter? Pretty fancy for an ex-con."

"I know that piece," said Planter shortly. "Wolfram's hymn to Venus, from *Tannhauser*."

*

It had started him thinking again. Gwen had played it so often on her violin. Played it and sung it. Those were the days he hadn't known she was married, down in her red-and-gold apartment in the Artists Quarter. He'd been sculpting her—she'd had the second best figure he ever saw. Then he found out about her husband, for the husband burst in upon them. The husband had tried to kill Planter, but Planter had killed the husband. And Gwen had sworn his life away.

"Check elapsed time," Disbro bade him.

"Fifty-eight days nine hours and fifty-four minutes point seven," rejoined Planter at once.

"Prompt, aren't you? We'll be on Venus before the sixty-fourth day." Planter saw Disbro shift over in his hammock. "I'm going to shave. Then eat."

Disbro turned a stud in the wall. His electric razor began to hum. Planter opened a locker-valve and brought forth his own rations—a package of concentrated solid, compounded of chocolate, meat extract, several vitamin agents. It would sustain him for hours, but was anything but a fill to his hunger. He chewed it slowly to make it last longer, and sipped from a snipe-nosed container of water, slightly effervescent and acidulated. A few drops escaped between snout and lip, and swam lazily in the gravityless air of the cabin, like shiny little bubbles.

"Planter," said Disbro, suddenly pleasant, "we're going to fool 'em."

He shut off his razor. Planter took another nibble. "Yes, Disbro?"

7

"We'll land at the north pole."

Planter shook his head. "We can't. This rocket is set at mid-point on the Venusian disk."

"We can. I've tinkered with the controls. A break for us, no break for the Foundationeers at home. They're watching us through telescopes. What they want is our crash on Venus, with a great upflare of the exploding fuel. Then they'll know that we landed, and can shake hands all 'round on a 'successful advancement.' But we're curving away, then in. I've fixed that. We'll not blow off and make any signal; but we'll live."

"North pole," mused Planter, pensively.

"No spin to Venus up there. We'll land solidly. We'll land where it's coolest, and none too cool. Her equator must be two degrees hotter than Satan's reception hall. The pole may be endurable."

"What then?" asked Planter.

"We'll live, I say. Don't you want to live?"

Planter hadn't thought about it lately. But suddenly he knew that he did want to live. His was a family of considerable longevity. His grandfather had attained the age of one hundred and seven, and had claimed to remember the end of the Second World War.

"Six days to study it over," Disbro was saying. "Then we'll have a try. If we land alive, we'll laugh. If we die trying, we'll have nothing to worry about. Float up here, will you? Take over. I'm going to have a little sleep."

*

Through choking steam, white and ever-swirling, drove the silvery cigar that was the ninth rocket ship to attempt to voyage across space. From its snout blossomed sudden flame, blue and red and blue again—rocket counter-blasts that were designed to act as brakes. They worked, somewhat. The speed cut from bullet-rate to falling-rate. From falling-rate to flying-rate. Then, of a sudden, partial clarity around it. Within an upper envelope of blinding vapors, Venus had a thinner atmosphere, partially transparent. Below showed a surface of fluffy greens, all sorts of greens—lettuce, apple, olive, emerald, spinach, sea greens. Vegetation, plainly, and lots of it. The ship, steadying in its plunge like a skilled diver, nosed across toward a wet, slate-dark patch that must be open ground. From the stern, where rocket tubes had ceased blazing, broke out a massive expanse of fabric—a parachute. Another and another. Down floated the craft, thudding, at last, upon its resting place.

Planter felt a cramping pain. He realized that to feel pain one must be alive. Then his head throbbed—it hung head downward. Gravity was back. He groped for his hammock fastenings, loosened them, and lowered himself to a standing position beneath, on the round port that had been forward. Disbro hung in his hammock, motionless but moaning faintly.

Planter hurriedly freed him and laid him flat on his back. He fumbled a locker open, brought out a water-pot. A little spurt between Disbro's short, scornful lips brought him back to consciousness.

"We made it," was Disbro's first comment, full of triumph and savagery. "Help me up. Thanks. Whoooh! We seem to have socked in somewhere, nose first."

He was right. No sign of light or open air showed through the forward port, nor the side ports from which Planter had been wont to study the reaches of space. Disbro looked up. The after bulkhead, now their ceiling, had a hatchway. "Hoist me," he said to Planter, who made a stirrup of his hands and obliged. The slightly lesser gravitational pull of Venus made Disbro more active than on Earth. He caught Planter's hammock, got his foot on a side-bracket for steadiness, and climbed up to the hatch. A tug at the clamps opened it, and he wriggled through.

"Wake up, you big buffalo," Planter heard him snarling. Max was evidently unconscious up there. Planter, without a helper to lift him, made shift by climbing Disbro's hammock, then his own, to gain the compartment above.

"He'd have died if he had an ounce of brains," commented Disbro, pointing. Max lay crumpled against the bulkhead, close to the great bank of levers he had been working. In his hands were grasped broken pieces of network from his hammock.

"He was out of the lashings when we landed," Disbro went on. "We were about to hit, and he grabbed hold. Must have passed out. But the big lump's single-minded—abnormally so. He hung on without knowing, and the breaking of those strands kept him from crashing full force."

Planter knelt and pulled Max straight. Max was tremendous, a burly troll in his coveralls. His shoulders were almost a yard wide, his hands like oversize gloves. His big face, with its broad jaw, heavy dark brows and ruddy cheeks, might have been handsome, was not the nose smashed in by a blow taken in some old ring battle.

"Don't waste water," cautioned Disbro as Planter hunted for the food-locker. "I'll bring him out of it." He knelt and slapped the inert face sharply.

Max's mouth opened, showing a gap where his front teeth had been beaten out. He gave a grumbling yell, then sprang erect so suddenly that Disbro, starting away, almost fell through the hatchway. Max saw Planter, scowled and snorted, then fell into a boxing stance. He inched forward, his mighty fists fiddling hypnotically.

"Time!" yelled Planter at once. "This isn't a fight, Max! We've landed—safe and alive—on Venus!"

Max's eyes widened a little. He grinned loosely, and pulled off his helmet. His skull was thatched with bushy, black hair. "Uhh," he said, in a deep, chiding tone. "I forgot. Uhhh."

"Forgot!" echoed Disbro scornfully. "He sounds as if he had the ability to remember."

Planter studied the ports in this compartment. They, too, were obscured by wet-looking grail soil. The ship must be well buried in the crust of Venus. What if it was completely submerged, a tomb for them? He glanced upward to another hatchway, one that would lead past the rocket engines.

"Don't go up," Max cautioned him throatily. "Hot up there."

"Brilliant," was Disbro's ill-humored rejoinder. "Max actually knows that the engines will be hot."

Planter clapped Max on the big shoulder. "It'll be all right," he reassured the giant. "Get me a wrench, will you? That long-shanked one for tightening tube-housings will do."

*

He scrambled up along the levers, which made a ladder of sorts. The hatch to the engines had to be loosened with the wrench. Beyond, as Max had sagely warned him, it was stiflingly hot. He avoided gleaming, sweltering tubes and housings, scrambling to where a four-foot circle of nuts showed in the bulkheading. This would be the plate that closed the central stern, among the rear rocket-jets. He began to loosen one.

"Stop that, you fool!" It was Disbro, who had climbed after him and was watching. "Who knows about this lower atmosphere of Venus?"

"I'm going to find out about it," replied Planter, a little roughly, for he did not like Disbro's manner. He gave the nut another turn.

"Wait, wait," cautioned Disbro. He climbed all the way into view, holding up a glass flask with a neck attachment of gauges and pipings. "I got a sample, through the lock-panel—plenty of air-bubbles were carried down with us. Let me work it out before you do anything heroic."

Disbro was right. He was usually right, about technologies. Planter mopped his brow on the sleeve of his coverall, and waited.

"Yes," Disbro was commenting. "Oxygen—nice article of that, and plenty. Nitrogen, too. Just like Earth. Quite a bit of carbon dioxide. It'll be from all that vegetation. Certified breathable. Go on and unship that plate."

Planter did so. He loosed the last net, and pushed against the plate. It stirred easily—the after part of the ship would still be in the open. Disbro, climbing after him, caught his elbow.

"I go out first," he announced. "They marked me down as senior of the expedition. One side."

Planter stared quizzically, and once again did as Disbro told him. The lean man thrust up the plate like a trapdoor, and crept out.

"At last!" he yelled back. "Men on Venus! Come on, Planter!"

Planter called back to Max, who was bringing up a bundle of articles Disbro had chosen for the venture outside—two repeating rifles, two pistols, several tools, and tins of food, coils of rope. Planter helped him with the load, and they got outside with it.

Disbro had slid down the step bulge of the hull. He clung to a grab-iron, his

11

feet just above the gray muck into which they had plunged. He stared up.

"First man to set foot on Venus," he was saying. "Who was second of you two?"

"We didn't stop to bother," Planter replied. "What now?"

He stared around, to answer his own question. Venus was dull, like a very cloudy day at home. The air was moist, but fresh, and little wreaths and veils of mist kept one from seeing far. But he made out that they had found lodgment in a sterile-looking clearing with a muddy floor that might or might not sustain a man's weight. All around was a crowded wall of vegetation—towering high above the range of his vision into upper fog, tight grown as a hedge, and vigorously fat of twig and leaf. Planter, no botanist, yet was aware at once of strangeness beyond his power to describe. He knew that specimens should be gathered and preserved to take home.

To take home? Home to Earth? But the ship was almost buried in this mud. He remembered Disbro's dry comment—"Our little gray home in the west." They were on Venus. Undoubtedly to stay.

Max, beside him, gave a sort of gurgling bellow of surprise and fear. "Uhhh! Something's got Mr. Disbro!"

*

For once, Max was being articulate. For once, Disbro was being silent.

Glancing down, Planter saw the slender, elegant figure writhed close against the metal hull, clutching with both hands the grab-iron. Disbro stared groundwards, and what could be seen of his face was as white as a wood-boring grub. One of his legs was drawn up, knee bracing upon the plates, the other stretched out grotesquely, as if to point a toe at something in the muck.

It took a second staring study to realize that a whiplike strand of something that gleamed and tightened was snapped around Disbro's ankle.

"Rope, Max," snapped Planter. He made a quick hitch around a rocket-tube, and lowered himself in a rush. His free hand grasped a heavy automatic pistol. He paused in his descent just above Disbro, studying the black, shiny tether.

It protruded from the semi-glutinous mud, which stirred and quivered around the protrusion. A sense was there of rigid grasp and slowly contracting pressure. It was squeezing the captured ankle, it was shortening itself to pull Disbro down. Disbro said nothing because he had caught his breath for an effort at wrenching free. But he could not do that. His strong, lean fingers were beginning to slip on the grab iron. He turned horror-widened eyes toward Planter.

"Hang on," muttered Planter, and aimed his pistol. No sure shot, he nevertheless was close to his target. He fired a .50 caliber slug, another and another. Two of them hit the tail, tentacle or proboscis.

At once it let go of Disbro, gesticulating wildly. Blood sprang forth on its shiny integument—Venusian blood was red, mused Planter, even as Venusian herbage was green. Disbro gave a choking gurgle that might have been thanks, relief or effort. A moment later he was swarming up Planter's rope like a monkey.

But Planter did not follow. The appendage he had wounded was drawing out of sight, like a worm into its hole; but two more just like it had fastened upon his foot and knee.

He lost his grip and fell into the mud. It was like a dip into thick gravy. The stuff lapped and closed over his head, and he let go of the pistol to try to swim. A couple of laborious strokes brought him back to the surface, gasping and blowing away thick lumps from nose and mouth. A moment later two more tentacles were groping and seizing at his shoulder and waist. Four bonds now tightened upon him, like lariats.

Planter seemed to be thinking in two compartments. One set of thoughts dictated his floundering, desperate struggle. The other considered the situation with a curiosity dispassionate and almost mild. The creature that snared him was just what he might have expected—something on the octopus order. How many science fiction stories had dealt with such monsters on strange worlds? The creepy writhings of tentacles appealed to fantasy writers—the neat, simple, active structure of the brute was logical to the great mechanic who devised Nature. The thing had him, in any case, if he could not kick or struggle or cut free.

Cut free! That was it. He had a knife, in the side pocket of his coveralls.

He dug for it, almost dropped it from his muddy fingers, then yanked open the biggest blade. He slashed at the nearest tentacle, the one around his waist. It parted like a cane-stalk before a machete. The other arms quivered and slackened, plainly shocked by pain. Planter rolled out of their grip, started to swim away anywhere.

He looked over his shoulder and saw his enemy as it humped itself partially into view.

Not such an octopus, after all.

The dispassionate part of Planter's brain called the thing an animated tall tree. The slender tentacles sprouted from a thicker trunk, that could curve and writhe and wallow, but not so readily. It was of a rubbery gray-brown, and at the upper end, nested among the tentacle-roots, was what must be its mouth. That mouth opened and shut in almost wistful hunger. Planter swam furiously. He wanted to reach and climb the stern of the rocket ship, but the thing knew his wish, and moved to head him off. He kicked and fought his way toward the far mass of leaves that bordered this mud-pit.

From among those leaves glowed for an instant a sort of splinter of yellow light. A small object sang over Planter's helmeted head like a bee, and struck behind him with a little *chock*. It must have found lodgment against the hall-tree thing, which paused in its pursuit to flop and spatter the mud with its tentacles. Planter blessed the diversion, whatever it was, and strove nearer to the shore.

The forest was alive, he suddenly decided. Out of its misty tangle a great leafy branch swung knowingly toward him. He clutched at it, brought away a fat, moist handful of strange-shaped leaves. His other hand made good its hold on the branch itself, and with the last of his strength he dragged himself to where roots hummocked above the mud.

Then he saw where the branch had come from. A slim, active figure stood among the stems, pressing with both hands upon the base of the branch to make it move into the open. As Planter scrambled to safety, the figure relaxed its helpful shoving, and the branch moved back toward the perpendicular.

14

Planter gazed in utter lost unbelief at this stranger.

It was a woman, young, fair, fine-limbed. She wore the briefest of garments, belted around with strange weapons, and her feet were shod in cross-gartered buskins. Upon her tumble of golden curls rode a metal helmet that reminded him of Grecian antiquity. Her bare arms, round but strong, cradled something with a stock and butt of a musket, but with a short, tight-strung bow at its muzzle—surely the pattern of a medieval crossbow.

Her face was of a flawless pink-and-white beauty, just now stamped with utter disdain. Its short, rosy mouth opened, and formed words.

Words that Planter understood!

"You fool," said the girl with the crossbow. "You scurvy fool."

*

Disbro, barely able to stir for shock and weariness, climbed only a few hand's breadths out of danger before he must stop and wheeze for breath. At last he could make himself heard:

"Max! You pighead, help me!"

"Uhh," came the grunt of assent from above, as the big fellow slid down in turn. He slipped a thick arm around Disbro, hoisting the tall, slender body as if it were a bundle of old clothes, and slid it across a shoulder like the jut of a crag. Then Max scaled the rope once again, to the safe top of the nosed-over rocket ship.

Disbro found his own feet, and shakily wiped his clear-cut face, still pale from exertion and terror. "That was close."

"Say," ventured Max, "Mr. Planter, he's gone."

Disbro looked around. The mud expanse around them was stirred up as if by boiling struggles, but there was no sign of Planter or the thing with the tentacles.

"That thing got him," decided Disbro, but Max shook his heavy head.

"Huh-uh," he demurred. "No. The girl, she got him."

"Girl?" echoed Disbro, and scowled.

"What girl?"

Max pointed with a finger like the haft of a hammer. "She was in the trees.

15

Got him."

Disbro peered at the trees, then at Max. His scowl deepened. "What are you drivelling about?"

"The girl," said Max.

Disbro snorted and skinned his teeth in scorn.

"How," he demanded of the misty skies, "do I get mixed up with minus quantities like this? A girl, the man says! Here on Venus!"

"A girl," repeated Max firmly.

Disbro wheeled upon him.

"Come off of that!" he commanded sharply. "Planter's gone. Dead. You're all I have to associate with. You'll act sane, whether you are or not."

Max's big, pained eyes faltered before the glittering accusation of Disbro's gaze. "All right," he conceded.

"There wasn't any girl there, you idiot!"

Max nodded. "I saw—"

"Shut up!" Disbro cut him off. "No girl, I said!"

"No girl," repeated Max obediently.

Rain began to fall, fat drops the size of marbles.

"Back inside," commanded Disbro. "There'll be lots of this kind of weather. We'll have something to eat, then study another way to reach the trees yonder."

"No girl," said Max. "But I saw."

*

The rain that drove Disbro and Max back into their shelter filtered through layers of leafage, beginning to wash the mud from Planter's clothing. He stared again at his rescuer.

"I seem to have understood what you said," he managed at last.

"Isn't so strange, that?" she flung back, in words somehow run together. "E'en though you're mad enow to sport with yonder muck-worm," and her wide, bright blue eyes flicked toward the danger he had lately avoided, "you'll have the tongue of mankind. Art no man?"

"Man enough, young woman," rejoined Planter, a little nettled. "I suppose it's like the fantasies—we can read each other's minds, or something."

"Something," she echoed, as if humoring a child.

"And I owe you thanks for saving my life."

"Oh, 'twas no great matter." She shouldered the crossbow. "Come, for the Skygors will be about our heels."

She picked her way rapidly among the steam, with the surest and cleverest of feet. Women on Earth were never so graceful or sure, decided Planter, hurrying after. He was aware that he did not step on the muddy surface of Venus, but upon a matted over-floor, of roots, fallen stems, ground-vines, sometimes great sturdy leaves like lily-pads grown to the size of double mattresses. "Wait, young lady," he called, "who are the Skygors, you mentioned and why should they be after us?"

She halted again, swung and studied him with more of that disdainful curiosity. "'Tis a gruel-brained idiot," she decided, as if to herself. "For that they cast him out. Methought 'twas strange that a man should flee, of himself, from sure shelter and victual."

It was raining harder. The great roof of vegetation only partially broke that downpour. It sluiced away the coating of mud from Planter, and soaked his stout garments through. He felt miserable in the dampness, but his girl guide throve, if anything, in the drops that struck and rolled down her bare arms and shoulders.

He saw, too, that she followed something of a trail among the stalks and stems. It was barely wider than his own stalwart shoulders could pass, and wound crazily here and there; but one must stick to it, for to right and left the jungle grew thicker than a basket. He called out again.

"Miss! Young lady!"

She turned, as before. "What now?"

"This path—what is it? Did you make it? Tell me things." He made a gesture of appeal, for she was putting on that look of contempt once more. "You see, I'm no more than an hour old on this planet—"

"Od so! Your brain is younger than that. Leave me, I have no time for idiots."

Abruptly she stiffened, widened her eyes, lifted a finger to her red lips for silence. The two of them stood close together in the misty rain, their ears sharpened. Planter heard what she had heard—a rustling, crunching approach, along some other angle of the jungle path.

The girl wrenched apart two sappy lengths of vine, and with a jerk of her head bade Planter slip through into the great thicket. He did so, and she followed. Turning, her lithe body close against his, she brought her crossbow to the ready.

"Danger?" whispered Planter, and she nodded bleakly.

The approach was coming near. Planter judged that whatever threatened them was two-legged, weighty, and great-lunged—many yards off, it wheezed like a faulty engine. His companion's ears were better than his, or more experienced. She gauged the nearness of the stranger, and the crossbow went to her shoulder like a rifle. Planter saw that it operated on a spring trigger that would trip a latch and release the string. The bow, violently recovering from its bending, would force the missile along a groove in the top of the stock. All parts—stock, bow, and string—were of some massive dark metal, apparently treated with grease to save it from the constant dampness. The missile itself was not an arrow, but seemed the size and shape of a silvery fountain pen. Planter burned to ask questions about it; but the enemy was in sight by now, something of mottled green and black that shouldered upright along the way between the thickets.

Planter felt his companion's body grow tense against his shoulder. Her finger touched the trigger lightly. The metal string twanged, and with a waspy hum the missile leaped toward its target. At the same time, a little burst of flame showed from it, bright yellow. *Chock!* the shot went home, as that other shot against the thing called a muck-worm.

Down floundered the green-spotted form. At once the girl was out of hiding, and stooping above her quarry.

Planter, following, peered with wonder and caution. He saw a body larger than himself, and grotesquely of the same build. A dumpy torso on massive back-bent legs like a cricket's; wide flapper feet, a round, low head with a

18

monstrous slash of mouth, big eyes now filming with death, no nose at all—the creature was very like a nightmare frog. But this frog wore garments, of linked and plaited metal wire and rubbery-looking fabric. It had a silver belt, with pouches and holsters. These pouches and holsters the girl was now plundering.

"Quick," she snapped at Planter over her rosy shoulder. "Take the spoil. He will have friends, and they must not find us."

*

Her tone was still reminiscent of Disbro speaking to Max. Planter's ravenous curiosity was at last completely overridden. "Young lady," he said flatly. "I'm not prepared to endure any more—"

She suddenly screamed, not like a warrior but like any girl who is mortally frightened.

Planter had the time to realize that she saw something just beyond him. He pivoted and set himself as another of the froggy beings charged.

"More Skygors!" he heard a cry behind him, and he knew that it was Skygors he faced.

Planter was a boxer of sorts, strong if not brilliant, and his unthinking reflex was to plant his feet, bend his knees, and crouch for attack or defense. That reflex shortened his height by several inches, and saved his life. The Skygors that rushed him had pointed a pistol-form weapon, from which came yellow flame as from the crossbow. A silvery object meant to scatter his brains only sang above his head with millimeters to spare. Before the pistol-like weapon could aim and spit again, Planter had charged in.

It was all he could do, but it was enough. He jabbed viciously with his left fist, followed with his right to the abdomen. The left knuckles slashed soft flesh about the wide mouth, his right hand almost broke on a hard belt-buckle. Both blows were staggering to the wheezing adversary, who dropped its pistol and yelled with a voice like a steam whistle. It made words, each of them almost deafening to Planter. To silence it more than anything else, Planter drove in closer still and lifted an uppercut as though it were a shovelful of gravel.

19

It found the point where a Terrestrial man would have a chin. Down floundered the clumsy body, and Planter, with no thought of referees or rules, set his heavy boot on the face and bashed it in. He stepped across the subsiding form, in time to encounter another.

This one got great flappy hands upon him. Their grip was knowing, powerful, wicked. The Skygor plucked him close, its mouth grinned into a gape. It had teeth, it was going to bite.

He was held by the shoulders, and doubted if he could break away. Instead of trying, he put his own hands to the thing's elbows, drew his right knee tight to his chest and planted a toe in a metal-clad midriff. Then, even as the open paw sought to seize his face, he threw himself backward. Landing flat on his shoulder blades, he drew down with his hands and hoisted with his feet.

His opponent somersaulted in air, and fell with a heavy squashing thump upon the root-tangled floor of the trail. In a flash, Planter was up. He jumped with both feet. Bones broke under the impact. A second Skygor was down—dead or dying—

"Aside!" the girl was calling, and he obeyed, flattening against a cross-weaving of vine stems. She was risen upon one knee, crossbow to shoulder. It twanged, flashed, and once again its successful charge sounded its *chock*. Planter glanced down the trail in time to see a fourth and last Skygor drop down.

He found that he was gasping for air, and trembling as though the danger were still to come instead of past. The girl rose, came to him, and touched his arm. She smiled, her eyes shone. Gone was the contempt, the superiority. She only admired, completely and frankly.

"Sink me, you're a fighter," she said. "Ecod! I saw only the flight of fists, and a Skygor went down, and another! You saved my life—and we have four Skygors to strip, with none to boom about where we went from here. Your name, friend?"

"Planter," he said. "David Planter."

"David Planter," she repeated. Her "A" was very broad, so that she made the name almost "Dyvid." Again she smiled. "A king's name, is't not? I am called Mara. Come, help me take what is valuable from this carrion."

Planter's heart warmed to her. "Thanks for your kind words," he smiled back. "But I did what any man would do."

"All men are slaves," she surprised him by saying. "You will amaze the other girl-warriors, when I bring you to the Nest."

*

Disbro, standing on the glass port-pane that was now floor for the control-room, labored and cursed at his keyboard. He pressed one, two, an octave. The nosed-over ship stirred, but did not rise.

"Max!" bawled Disbro to the upper hatch. "Pressure!"

"Giving you all there is," Max informed him timidly.

Disbro turned from his controls, shrugging in disgust.

"Those bow-tubes are jammed or displaced," he cursed. "We can't clear off till we get her up and clean them—and we can't get her up and clean them until they work. Huhh!"

Max's big, diffident face framed itself in the hatchway, registering a small hope.

"We're floating," he volunteered. "Close to those trees and things."

Disbro showed interest. "Then we'll get our feet on solid ground, or nearly solid. That tentacle-thing won't be sloshing around." He beckoned. "Come down."

Max obeyed. From a locker Disbro took a pressure squirt of waterproofing liquid. He sprayed Max's clothes, then his own. "That'll shed rain," he said. "Buckle on a pistol, if you're smart enough to use one. And give me two."

Once more the hammocks in the lower chamber, and the levers in the higher, gave them a ladder-way up. Disbro, emerging first into the damp, warm mist, saw at once that they had visitors.

The ship, as Max said, floated close to the mat of growth that fringed the muddy pool. Here the jungle consisted of meaty stems, straight, thick and close-set, with tangled fermiform foliage. A little above mud-level, gnarled roots wove into a firm footing, and upon it, pressing from the thickets toward the ship, were huge biped creatures in gleaming metal harness.

These had chopped down spongy trunks and branches, on which to venture over the mud-surface as on rafts. Coming near the ship, they had passed cables of grease-clotted metal wire around it, mooring it fast to thicker trunks. As Disbro stared down, several of them began to converse in tones that rang and boomed like great gongs. Half-deafened, Disbro still could perceive that their voices had inflection and sense. Harness, concerted action, tools, a language—here was a master race, comparable to Terrestrial humanity.

One of them turned a bulging black eye upward, and saw Disbro. Its flat face split across, and a mouth like an open Gladstone bag shouted its discovery. One green paw, webbed but prehensile, snatched a weapon from a metal-linked waist belt, and aimed it at the Terrestrial.

But Disbro, too, was quick on the draw. His gang-rule on Earth had necessitated shooting skill as well as leadership. His own automatic sprang into his hand. "No, you don't!" he snapped, and shot the weapon out of the Venusian's flipper.

It screamed in a voice that vibrated the steamy air, and its companions started and shrank back in startled wonder. Disbro drew a second pistol, leveling it at them.

"I'll shoot the first one that moves," he promised, as if they could understand; and understand they did. Up went shaky flipper-hands.

"No! No!" they boomed in thunderous humility. "Don't! Don't!"

He had not the time to wonder that they spoke words he knew. He swung his weapons in swift arcs, covering them all. Max, behind, had sense enough to level the long barrel of a repeating rifle. "Please!" roared a Venusian who seemed to be a leader. "We do naught to you!"

"Better not," cautioned Disbro loftily. "We're more profitable as friends than as enemies."

"Friends!" agreed the leader. "Friends!"

"If you try any funny business—" went on Disbro. "Well, watch!"

He snapped his right-hand gun up and fired. The bullet snipped away a leaf the size of an opened umbrella. As the great green blob drifted down, Disbro fired again and again, until, ripped to rags, the leaf fell limply among the Venusians. They moaned, like awe-struck fog horns.

"Understand?" taunted Disbro. "Savvy? I could kill you all as easy as look at you."

"Friends!" promised the leader again.

"Max," muttered Disbro, "these birds quit very easily without a fight. But keep me covered from up here."

Planter's rope still dangled along the hull. Disbro slid down, coming to his feet on the raft-heap below. The Venusians gave back in wary confusion. Disbro allowed himself to smile upward.

"See what an ape you are, Max?" he chuckled. "You got a look at one of these, and thought it was a girl! You're not much of a picker, Max."

To the Venusian chief he said: "I think I'll muscle in on your territory."

*

Mara, the crossbow-girl, brought Planter to the place she called the Nest.

It was hollowed out in the thickest part of the towering jungle, as a rabbit's form is hollowed among tall grasses. The floor was of plaited and pressed withes, supported on stumps and roots of many tall growths. Rounding upward and outward from this were walls, also of wooden poles and twigs, woven into the growing tangle. The roof was similarly made, but strengthened and waterproofed with earth, dried and baked by some sort of intense heat.

The space thus blocked off was shaped like the rough inside of a hollow pumpkin, and in size was comparable to the auditorium of a large theater. Within it were set up smaller huts and bowers. There were common cooking-fires, in ovens of stone and mud-brick, and a great common light suspended from the ceiling by a long heavy chain. This was a metal lamp, fed by oily sap from some sort of tree.

Finding the Nest was difficult. Mara had picked a careful way through mazes of thick vegetation, paying special attention to the rearranging of leaves and branches behind them. Sagely she explained that the Skygors, when hunting her kind, were thus completely lost. Even at the very doorstep of the

Nest, the tangled vines, branches and leaf-sprays obscured any hint of such a place at hand.

The dwellers in the Nest were all women.

They came cautiously forward, twenty or so, as Mara ushered Planter inside. They were active specimens, dressed scantily and attractively, like Mara. Most of them were young, several comely. All were fair of skin and hair, a logical condition in the cloudy air of Venus. They wore daggers, hatchets, ammunition pouches. Even at home, they all carried crossbows.

"What does this man here?" demanded a lean, harsh-faced woman of middle age. "Is he not content with servitude?"

Mara shook her head. "He's like none we know. He fights more fiercely than we—Ecod, shouldst have seen him! Bare-handed, he o'ercame two Skygors. I slew two more. Look at our trove!"

She opened a parcel of great leaves, and showed dozens of the silver pens that were ammunition for both the Skygor pistols and the human crossbows. Planter also showed what he had brought from the battlefield—several belts, numerous harness fastenings, and two of the guns. These latter made the crossbow-girls nervous.

"We stand by these," Mara said, tapping her crossbow.

Planter fiddled with a pistol. Its mechanism was strange but understandable, and he flattered himself that he could learn to use it. As for the pen-missiles, they seemed to contain a charge that burned violently on exposure to air. The trigger-mechanism, whether of pistol or crossbow, punctured it, set it afire, and the vehemence of combustion not only propelled it but destroyed the target completely.

The older woman, whose name was Mantha, nodded her head over a decision.

"Let the man have the dag," she granted, with an air of authority. "If he fights as Mara says, he may be of aid. Yet he is unlike those we know, in hue and aspect."

True enough, Planter was dark of complexion, with black curls and ruddy tan jaws. He spoke to Mantha, respectfully, for the others called her

"Mother" and treated her as a commander.

"I'm not of your people," he said. "I come from another planet. Earth."

"Earth?" she repeated. "You come from there? Why, so do we all."

*

Down a trail went a patrol of Skygors. Among them, not much under them in size, tramped Max. His broad shoulders bore a great burden of supplies from the ship. At the head of the procession, next to the chief, walked Disbro.

As someone else was saying to Planter at almost the same moment, the chief Skygor boomed to Disbro: "You are not like men we know."

"Naturally not," agreed Disbro. "Your race is more like a bunch of freak reptiles."

"Not my race," demurred the chief Skygor. "Men. Slaves."

Disbro understood only part, and took exception to that. "I'm no slave of yours," he warned.

"No. Equal. We have long needed equal men, to kill off the wild girls."

"You see, Mr. Disbro?" chimed in Max from behind.

*

David Planter was embarrassed.

Inside the Nest, he sat on a crude chair opposite Mantha, the Mother. The overhead light burned dim, and damp-banishing fires in the ovens mingled red glows. Planter asked questions, but was distracted by the crossbow-girls, who watched him with round eyes, whispering and giggling. Mara, near by, scowled at the noise-makers.

"This Venus world has much that's unknown," Mantha said. "Here in the north can we dwell. Not many days off the steam is thick, the heat horrid, the jungle dreadful. None go there and return."

"Mother, if you are called that, enlighten me," begged Planter. "You say you come from Earth."

"Our fathers came. Lifetimes agone."

Planter's good-looking face showed his amazement. Interworld flight was new, he had thought. But some unknown expedition might have tried it,

25

succeeded, and then never returned to report.

"'Twas for fear of black Cromwell," Mantha enlarged.

"Cromwell!" echoed Planter. "The Puritan leader who fought and wiped out the English Cavaliers?"

Mantha seized on one word. "Cavaliers. Yes. Our lives were forfeit. We flew hither."

It explained everything—human beings in a world never meant for anything but amphibians, their fair complexions, their quaint but understandable speech, the crossbows that would be familiar weapons to Shakespere, Drake or Captain John Smith. Yes, it explained everything, except how pre-machine age Britishers could succeed on a voyage where eight space-ships before Planter's had failed.

"How did you fly?" demanded Planter, amazed.

Mantha shook her graying locks. "Nay, I know not. 'Twas long ago, and all records are held in the Skygor fastness."

"They stole from you?"

"After our fathers made landfall, there was war," Mantha said, her voice bitter. "The Skygors were many, and would have slain all, but thought to hold slaves. And as slaves our fathers dwelt and died, and their children after them."

"But you aren't slaves," protested Planter.

"'Tis Skygor fashion to keep all men, and such women as are hale enow for toil. Others who seem weak they cast forth to die, like us!"

"Who did not die," chimed in Mara, plucking her bowstring. "We found fruits, meat, shelter, and joined. Now we slay Skygors for their metals and shot. Lately they slay weaklings, lest they join us."

Planter whistled. This was a harsh proof of human tenacity. The Skygors discarding unprofitable servants and finding them a menace. "None of you are weaklings," he said.

"Freedom brings health," replied Mantha sentiously. "Yet they are many more than we, well fortified, and have a strange spell to whelm those who attack." She grimaced in distaste. "We but lurk and linger, fighting when we

MANLY WADE WELLMAN

must and fleeing when we may. As the last of us dies—"

Things began to happen.

A tall, robust girl, very handsome, had been hitching her woven chair close to Planter. With a pert boldness she touched his hand.

"I've seen no man since I was driven forth, a child," she informed him. "I like you. I am Sala."

Mara rose from her own seat, swore a rather Elizabethan oath, and slapped Sala's face resoundingly.

Sala, too, sprang up. Larger than Mara, she clutched her assailant's shoulders and tripped her over a neatly extended foot. Mara spun sidewise in falling, broke Sala's hold, came to her feet with a drawn dagger.

This happened silently and swiftly, with none of the screaming and fumbling that marks the rare battles between Terrestrial women. Planter stared, half aghast and half admiring. Another girl whispered behind him: "Let them fight, send them ill days! Look at me, I am not ugly."

Perhaps to flee this new admirer, Planter threw himself between the two fighters. As Mara attempted to stab Sala, Planter caught her weapon wrist and wrenched the knife from her. Meanwhile, Sala snatched up a crossbow. Leaving Mara, Planter struck the thing out of aiming line just in time. The pen-missile tore through the baskety wall of the Nest, and Planter gained possession of the crossbow, not without trouble.

"Are you girls fighting over me?" he demanded.

"Egad, what else?" challenged Mantha, who had also sprung forward. "Art a man of height and presence. For any man these my manless girls would contend."

"Aye, would we," agreed one of the bevy, with frightening candor.

"He's mine," snapped Mara, holding her own crossbow at the ready. "Step forth who will, and I speak true."

"I'm nobody's," exploded Planter. "Anyway, I'm going—I've two friends near here that I've got to find, and soon!"

"More men!" ejaculated Sala, forgetting her anger.

"Fighters, with weapons," said Planter, ignoring her. "They'll help you

27

smoke out these Skygors and set free your kinsmen."

Happy cries greeted his words.

"I'll guide you home, David Planter," offered Mara, and Mantha gestured approval.

Mara and Planter left the Nest by a new jungle trail. Mara explained that these tunnels were made by great floundering beasts, and served as runways for smaller land life. The girl trod the green, fog-filled labyrinths with assurance. Within minutes they reached the pool where Disbro had landed the ship.

At the edge floated the limp, dead thing that Mara had killed to save Planter. Small flutterers, like gross-winged flies but as large as gulls, swarmed to dig out morsels. Mara called the creature a krau, the flying scavengers ghrols. "Skygor words, for ugly beasts," she commented. "Neither is good for food."

Planter picked his way from root to root toward the ship. "Disbro!" he called. "Max!"

There was no answer. He scrambled up and inside, then out again. "Something's happened," he said gravely.

Mara studied the massed logs that made a rough raft. "Skygor work. And eke the rope of wires about your ship."

"They've been captured by Skygors? For slaves?" Planter had climbed down again. His hand sought the Skygor pistol at his belt, his face was tense and pale. "I'll get them back. Where's this swamp-city you mention?"

She pointed. "Not far. But the way is perilous. The trails throng with Skygors, and there is the spell."

"That sounds like some old superstition," snorted Planter. "I'm not afraid of Skygors. I killed two today."

"Aye," she smiled. "They are not great fighters in these parts. But there are more than two at the city ... come along."

"You can go back to the Nest."

She smiled more broadly. "How else will you find the way, my David? For you *are* my David."

"Don't start that again," he bade her, more roughly than he felt. "Lead the way."

*

Mara took a nearby jungle trail. After some time, she paused and studied the matted footing. "Tracks," she pronounced. "Certain Skygors, and two pairs of feet shod like yours."

Planter looked at the muddled marks thus diagnosed by the skilled trail-eye of Mara. "My friends and their captors?"

"Aye, that. They went this way. Come."

She slipped aside through the close-set stems. Planter did likewise. Mara slung her crossbow behind her, and climbed a trunk as a beetle scales a flower-stalk. "'Tis safer from Skygors up here," she told him over her shoulder "Follow me carefully."

Planter did so, with difficulty. He was a vigorous climber, and the lesser gravity of Venus made him more agile. But Mara, some forty feet overhead, swung through the criss-cross of limbs and vines like a squirrel. "Wait!" he called, striving to catch up.

She paused, finger to lips. As he came near, she said softly: "Not so loud! We come close. Feel you the spell?"

Hanging quietly, Planter did feel it.

Uneasiness came, chilling his back despite the steamy warmth. His hair stirred on his head, his teeth gritted, and he could not reason himself out of the mood. Mara moved ahead, and he followed. Growing accustomed to the climbing, he made progress. But the uncomfortable sense of peril grew rather than diminished.

Once in their strange journey Mara paused, and from a belt-pouch produced food. It consisted of fire-dried fruits, strange to Planter but tasty and substantial; also two meat-dumplings, made by wrapping a nut-flavored dough around morsels of flesh. For drink she plucked long spear-like leaves from a vine, and Planter found them full of pungent juice. While they munched, he heard boomings in the distance, which Mara identified as Skygor speech.

"We are almost there," she whispered. "Look well."

She rose, and again they took up the journey. After a time she paused again, and pointed.

Just beyond them the branches thinned out over a great open space in the jungle. Under a far-flung canopy of white vapors lay the swamp-city of the Skygors.

*

Planter, gazing in wonder at the strange city, thought of old Venice, or of a beaver colony in a diked pond. Before and beneath him was a quiet greeny-clear body of water. Around its rim grew shrubs, bushes and huge reeds, their roots clasping the great facing of white rock which apparently paved the banks and bottom of the pool. In the water itself, poking above the surface in little pointed clusters and plainly visible where they extended beneath, were the houses of the Skygors.

They were of some kind of soil or clay that had been processed to a concrete hardness, and were tinted in various colors. Some of the smaller dwellings were roughly spherical, and crowned with cone-shaped roofs. Others, larger, protruded well above the water in cylindrical form. Here and there travel-ways connected the clustered groups.

But it was beneath the surface that the town was complex and great. It seemed to lie tier above tier, closely built and grouped, with here and there protruding arms or wings of building, like coral budded from the main mass. In those depths swam myriads of Skygors, plainly at home under water. More of them, at the window-holes of the upper towers or paddling on the surface, boomed and roared to each other in their deafening language. From on high, Planter saw them as smaller and less to be dreaded. They might have been slight fantasy things, water-elves or super-intelligent frogs.

"Look you, David Planter," prompted Mara, at his elbow.

From a tunnel-like hole in the jungle, a group of Skygors emerged. Among them were two human figures, clad like Planter in loose overalls and helmets.

"Your friends?" Mara questioned.

"Right," snapped Planter grimly. He drew the pistol-weapon and glared.

Disbro and Max, the latter stooping under a great bale of goods from the ship, had paused on the brink of the water. A Skygor was thundering to them, in words of English which Planter, across the water, found hard to catch. Other Skygors motioned at the pool, and one or two jumped in and struck out for nearby buildings.

"They want your friends to dive," Mara informed him. "See, the slim one shakes his head."

Planter rested the pistol on his forearm, and sighted on the Skygor who harangued Disbro. Meanwhile, other Skygors were bringing up what appeared to be a small, inflated boat, that operated with a paddle-wheel arrangement behind.

Mara saw what Planter was doing. "No!" she gasped. "Don't, David!"

"I'm going to," he told her.

"We'll be next!"

"Nonsense! Those flapper-footed devils can't climb! They're too heavy, too clumsy!"

She caught at his weapon wrist, but he had fired.

The Skygor weapon was a wondrous one. Even an indifferent shot like Planter could not miss with it. The Skygor beside Disbro seemed to burst into flame around his flat, bushel-mouthed face, and then he collapsed and lay still. His companions swarmed to his side, rending the air with their horrid yells.

Planter chuckled, and Mara moaned. The man moved forward among the branches, to a place where he could be seen.

"Hai, Disbro!" he trumpeted, as loudly as any Skygor. "Max! It's David Planter! Run while you have the chance, I'll pick those toads off!"

But neither of his friends offered to escape. They only stood and gazed at him.

"You idiots!" blazed Planter, and then saw that two of the Skygors on the inflated boat were aiming weapons at him. He sent a silver pen at their craft, and it melted abruptly as its air escaped from the puncture. A third shot took one of the Skygors splashing in the water. "Run, you two!" Planter bade his companions once more.

He felt a grip on his ankle, and glanced down. Mara had crouched low, was trying to pull him back from view. As soon as she had his eye, she let him go, and thrust both fingers into her ears in some sort of a sign he did not comprehend.

Understanding dawned suddenly, and too late.

The mist trembled and swirled at a sudden outburst of sound louder than even a Skygor chorus. Planter dropped his weapon, began to lift his hands to his ears in imitation of Mara. But he could not!

The noise possessed him, as a rush of electric current might course through a body, paralyzing and agonizing it. He swayed and floundered among the branches. His hair bristled, his ears rang, his blood coursed, every fiber of him vibrated. Yet something about it was vaguely familiar, as though it was something he had experienced, or a magnification of such a something.

Yes, of course ... the uneasiness that Mara called the "spell." Some device made a noise-vibration, normally sub-audible but unpleasant enough to warn aliens away. In a time like this, when attack came, it could be intensified to the point of striking the enemy stupid.

Meanwhile, he was falling, through branches and leafage, to splash clumsily into the water of the pool. Abruptly the noise ceased. The Skygors were around him, their flipper-hands fastening upon him, and he was too wrung out, too grateful for silence, to resist.

*

He may have fainted. Later on, he could not be sure. But his next clear memory was of lying in one of the inflated paddle-boats, in which sat Skygors with weapons. There also sat Disbro, watching him intently.

"Disbro!" muttered Planter. "They got you, too?"

"No, they didn't get me, too," mimicked Disbro. "I'm in the racket with them, understand?"

Planter sat up, and two Skygors half-drew their weapons to warn him. "I thought you were captured," he mumbled.

"Not me. I do things neatly. Showed I could be an enemy, but would rather

32

be a friend. You butted in, killing two of them. Someone says you got two others earlier today. They're holding you a prisoner, and probably you'll be killed."

Planter studied Disbro. "Easy does it," he said softly. "Better not act as if you know me. You might get mixed up in—"

"No chance!" snarled Disbro. "I told them that you were an enemy of mine. I'm not mixed up in anything."

Planter subsided. Plainly Disbro was able to take care of himself. Plainly Planter must do the same, with no help from anyone. He wondered about Mara, with a sudden chilled pang. The brave girl had guided him here, despite her knowledge that Skygor country was dangerous. She had done it to please him, because she liked him. He wondered what had happened to her.

He lounged under the Skygor guns, thinking of Mara. In his mind he saw the light of her steady blue eyes, felt the touch of her slim, strong hand. His heart quickened.

"Hang it," he told himself, "you aren't in love with her. She's a savage, and you only met her a few hours ago! You're only worried because you feel responsibility."

But he knew he lied.

The boat brought them to an entrance-hole at water-level, in a large cylindrical structure. Disbro swaggered inside, with his new friends. A guard prodded Planter with his pistol-barrel to follow. As Planter obeyed, he saw behind him another boat, in which rode Max with all the baggage he had been carrying. Skygors sat with Max, plainly on good terms. Max saw Planter, too, and his face twitched and scowled as in an effort to rationalize.

Inside, he found himself in a large bare room with dry, rough-cast walls. Disbro waited there, with a Skygor whose elaborate chain-mail suggested that he was an officer.

"Disbro," boomed this individual cordially, "You say this is your enemy? What shall be done to him?"

"I leave that to you, Phra," answered Disbro, with the grand manner of bestowing gifts. "You have your own ways of handling such problems. I am content."

Another Skygor approached, and the officer discussed the case in deafening Skygor language. Then, facing Planter, he resumed English:

"Your life is forfeit, but you look strong. Perhaps you can prove yourself worth keeping. Join the slaves."

He struck his webbed hands together. A human man ran in.

Like Mara and the other crossbow-girls, this man was blond, but the resemblance ended there. He wore loose, brief garments of elastic fabric, no weapons, and his face was mild and servile. Phra pointed to Planter.

"Below with him! Put him to the spring mill!"

The slave beckoned, and led Planter away, studying him curiously.

Planter spoke at once: "You have many friends here, in slavery? Perhaps I can get you out of this."

"Out of this!" The echo was horrified. "To starve in the jungle? Marry, sir, art mad or sick to say such a thing! Come, down these stairs."

*

Planter obeyed his new companion. They went down a dim, stone stairway, lighted with green bulbs. From below came sounds of mechanical action.

"What's your name?" Planter asked the slave.

"Glanfil. And you?"

"David Planter. How many slaves are there here? Human slaves?"

"Two hundred, belike. Half as many as the Skygors."

That was a new thought to Planter. On Earth, races were numbered in the millions—here, by the scores. Of course, this might not be the only Skygor city. Mara had mentioned the difficulty of exploring any distance from this habitable pole. For a moment he felt the thirst for knowledge. Wasn't this world as large as his own planet? Might it not have continents, oceans, mountain ranges, whole genera of strange species, perhaps other civilizations and climates? Then he remembered. He was a slave. And a booming voice drove the memory home.

"Below, men," thundered a Skygor guard. "You are not fed and lodged to be idle."

"Pardon," mumbled Glanfil, and quickened his descent. Planter followed, beating down a rage of battle at the rough shouting of the guard.

The under-water levels were not flooded, though the walls were gloomily damp. Planter found himself in a great rambling chamber, bordered and cumbered with machines, at which men toiled. Glanfil was presenting him to a Skygor, who made notes with a crayon-like instrument on a board. "New?" he questioned in his ear-dulling roar. "Whence came he? Never stop to answer—show him how to work your machine."

Glanfil led him to a cylindrical appliance against a wall. It had a multitude of levers and push-buttons, and lights shone in its glassed forefront. Most of these were green, but one turned red as they approached. Glanfil pushed a button and turned a lever. The light switched to green again.

"The red means a faulty rhythm somewhere in the light system," explained Glanfil. "Fix it by manipulating the buttons and levers near the red lights—yes, so. It takes not skill, but wary watching."

Planter took over. He found time to observe the rest of the slave-teemed basement.

Some operated a treadmill, others wound at keys or turned cranks. The machines were strange but not mysterious. He judged that they pumped, elevated, and modelled. Glanfil answered his questions:

"'Tis the Skygor method. We supply power by our labors. Springs, levers, such things, are worked."

"Springs and levers?" repeated Planter. "Is this a clockwork town? Why not fuel? Steam?"

Glanfil shook his head. "We men make small fires, but the Skygors not. Their nature is moist, they want such things not. As you say, clockwork is the use of this place."

"If you refuse to do this slave work, what then?"

Glanfil shrugged, and shuddered. "If the sin is not too great, you go to a level below this. Men drag upon a capstan, to wind the mightiest of springs for town works."

"Like rowing in a galley!" Planter summed up wrathfully. "But if the sin is pretty sinful?"

A Skygor overseer came close, saw that Planter had learned the simple machine, and called Glanfil to some other task. Planter worked until such time as a raucous voice bade another shift take over. Marshalled with twenty or more slaves, he was led away to a musty vault, one side of which was lined with cell-like sleeping quarters. Here was a brick oven—perhaps those in the Nest were designed from it—over which two sturdy women toiled at cookery. As the slaves entered, these women quickly passed out stone plates and metal spoons. Into these were poured generous portions of hot, appetizing stew.

"They feed you well, these Skygors," commented Planter to Glanfil as he finished his plateful.

"'Tis their fashion. They seek to make us happy."

Planter went to the kettles for another helping of stew, and ate more slowly. "I'd rather eat in freedom," he commented, half to himself.

"Freedom?" echoed Glanfil, as if scornful. "We hear of what freedom can be. Scant commons, rough beds, danger and damp. Better to toil honestly and fare well."

"Aye," said a bigger slave, with a spade beard of reddish tinge. "Did not the Skygors help our first fathers, stranger, as now they help you?"

"I've heard otherwise," Planter rejoined. "It seems there was a fight—the men were licked—the survivors made captive and put to work. That's what happened to me."

"Best be silent," murmured Glanfil, bending close. "That talk makes few friends."

*

Planter changed the subject, asking various questions about Venus. His companions eyed him strangely as he displayed his ignorance, but made cheerful answer.

The noise that had overwhelmed him was a vibrating metal instrument, they said. Their description made it sound like an organ of sorts. As he had surmised, it was always in some sort of operation, and could be turned on full force if need be. The Skygors, with senses meant to endure great noises, were not hurt by such a din, but human ears would be tortured if not quickly closed. "Our labors give the instrument power," informed Glanfil, rather proudly.

Planter thought over his experiences of the day. "The Skygors have many human devices," he ventured.

"Aye, that," agreed the big bearded one. "In the first days, our fathers brought many articles, which the Skygors developed and used."

"There's what I'm driving at!" Planter broke in, forgetting Glanfil's council to be cautious. "They not only enslaved you, they took your ideas and improved themselves. I'll wager they were savages to begin with! And you're actually grateful for the chance to crawl at their big, webbed feet!"

"This world belongs to the Skygors," spoke up one of the women as she washed dishes. "Without them we would be shelterless and foodless, like the weaklings they drove forth."

Planter refrained to tell what he knew of the crossbow-girls. Plainly he was up against an attitude of content from which it would be hard to free his new companions—harder than to free them from guards and prison walls.

He slept that night in a hammock-like bed, and next day worked at the machine. His toil was long, but not sapping, and food was good. Once a Skygor came to take his clothing, shoes and possessions, giving him a sleeveless shirt and shorts instead. Otherwise he was not bothered by the masters of the city. For days—perhaps ten—he followed this routine, masking his feeling of revolt.

Then came a Skygor messenger to lead him away along under-water corridors to someone who had sent. At the end of the journey he entered an office. There sat the person he least expected to see.

Disbro.

"You rat," Planter began, but Disbro waved the insult aside.

"Don't be a bigger ape than usual," he sniffed. "I've been able to do you a favor."

"You didn't do me much of a one when I was captured," reminded Planter.

"How could I?" argued Disbro, in the charming fashion he could sometimes achieve. "I was only on probation. If I'd tried to help you then, we'd both be dead, instead of both on top of this Turkish Bath world. Sit down." They took stools on opposite sides of a heavy, wooden table. "Planter, how would you like to help me run Venus?"

"You're going to get away from these Skygors?"

Again Disbro waved the words away. "Why should I? I'll run them, too. Look, we landed safely, didn't we? Observations on Earth will show that, won't they?"

"Right," agreed Planter, mystified. "There'll be more ships coming, to look for us and maybe set up a colony."

"That's it. We'll ambush those ships."

"Ambush?" repeated Planter sharply. "Losing your mind, Disbro?"

"No. I'm only thinking for all of us. Ships will come, I say. Loaded with supplies, valuables all sorts of things. We can overwhelm them as they land. Some of their crews will join us—the others can be rubbed out. And the law can't touch us, Planter! Not for a minute!"

"What are you driving at?" Planter demanded.

"I'm the law," said Disbro, tapping his chest. "Just now I string with the Skygors. Later I may knock 'em off. But anyway, I'm the commander of the first expedition to land on Venus. I have a right to take possession, in my own name." He got up, his voice rising clear and proud. "Possession, like Columbus! Not of a continent—of a whole world!"

*

Planter, leaning forward on his stool, clutched the edge of the table so strongly that his knuckles whitened.

"And what," he asked slowly and quietly, "do you want me to do?"

"I'm coming to that," said Disbro, smiling with superior craftiness. "You're going to help me solidify these loud-mouthed Skygors."

"They hold me for a slave," reminded Planter harshly, for he did not like the life as well as Glanfil and the others who toiled among the clockwork. But Disbro brushed the complaint aside.

"That's because they don't know what I know. Your lady friends, I mean."
Planter glanced up sharply. Disbro chuckled.

"I talk a lot with these Skygors. Not bad fellows, if you muffle your ears. Anyway, they tell me about a herd of wild girls that bushwacks them constantly, and which they hope I'll find and destroy. Lately some of those girls have been scouting around, yelling for something. The Skygors haven't the best of English, and don't know what the words mean. But I do. Those girls are calling your name. David Planter."

Mara had come back for him, then. She braved the terrors of the Skygor fortress, trying to get him back. Planter felt warmth around his heart. He faced Disbro and shook his head.

"I don't know what you're talking about," he said. "You must be getting drunk with your Skygor friends."

"They don't have any kind of liquor, only some sort of sniff-powder I wouldn't touch. And you're a cheerful liar, Planter. You know all about those girls, and you're probably good friends with them. Don't be a fool, I'm offering you a slice of my empire!"

"Empire!" echoed Planter, honestly scornful. "You really think you'll go through with this idea of grabbing Venus for yourself?"

"I know all the angles. Back on Earth I was boss of quite an organization."

"And ended up in jail, buying your way out by gambling your life on this voyage!" Planter rushed those words into speech, but made them clear, biting and passionate. "You're a case for brain doctors, not jail wardens. I don't know why I listen to you."

"I know why," hurled back Disbro. "Because I'm already quite a pet among these Skygors. I can kill you or save you. Meanwhile, we're changing the subject. I want you to lead me to these wild girls, and after we're solid with them, a bunch of Skygors will come—"

"Nothing doing!"

"In other words, you now admit that there is such a group! And you'll take orders, Planter. I'm still chief of the expedition."

Planter shook his head. "I can give you arguments on that. You've betrayed the trust of the Foundation back home. That lets you out. You don't have authority over me."

He rose abruptly. "Send me back to the basement, Disbro."

Disbro, too, jumped up. He held something in his hand. It was a gun, not a Skygor curiosity but a Terrestrial-made automatic.

"You don't get off that easy, Planter. I need you badly. And you need your insides badly. Knuckle down, before I blow them out!"

Planter smiled, broadly and rather sunnily. Suddenly he lifted a toe. He kicked over the table against and upon Disbro. Down went the elegant, lean figure, and a bullet sang over Planter's head as he dived in to grapple and fight.

Disbro, the lighter of the two, was wondrously agile. Almost before he struck the concrete floor, he was wriggling clear of the table. Planter's weight threw him flat again, but he struck savage, choppy blows with the pistol he still held. Half-dazed, Planter could not get a tight grip, and Disbro got away and up. Planter, shaking the mist from his battered head, staggered after him, caught his weapon wrist and wrung the gun away. It clanged down at their feet.

"All right, Planter, if you want it that way," muttered Disbro savagely, and took a long stride backward. He got time to fall on guard like the accomplished boxer he was.

Planter sprang after him. Disbro met him with a neat left jab, followed it with a hook that bobbed Planter's head back, and easily slid away from a powerful but clumsy return. When Planter faced him again, he stood out of danger, smiling and lifting a little on his toes.

"How do you like it?" he laughed. "Didn't know I was a fancy Dan, eh?"

Planter charged again. Disbro slipped right and left tries at his jaw, returned a smart peg to Planter's belly, and then let the bigger man blunder past and fetch up against a wall. Planter was forced to lean there a nauseous moment, and Disbro hooked him hard under the ear. A moment later, Planter was crouching and backing away, sheltering his bruised head with crossed arms. He heard Disbro laugh again. "This is fun," pronounced

Disbro. "I've been taught by professionals, Planter. Good ones, not washouts like poor Max."

Planter clinched at last, but Disbro's wiry body spun loose. The two faced each other, and Planter felt some of his strength and wit come back.

He realized that he was being beaten. He must change tactics. He remembered what he could of fist-science, and abruptly crouched. Again he advanced, but not in a rush. Inch by inch he shuffled in, head sunk between his shoulders, hands lifted to strike or defend.

"You look like a turtle," mocked Disbro, and tried with a left. It glanced off of Planter's forehead, and Planter sidled to his left, away from Disbro's more dangerous right. Bobbing and weaving lower still, he baffled more efforts to sting him. A moment later, Disbro was backing, and Planter had him in a corner, close in.

He struck, not for Disbro's adroit head, but for his body. His left found the pit of the stomach, just within the apex of the shallow, inverted V where ribs slope down from breastbone. Disbro grunted in pain, and Planter put all his shoulders behind a short, heavy peg under the heart. Again to the belly, twice—thrice—he felt Disbro sag. A hook glanced from Planter's jowl, but it was weak and shaky. Disbro managed to slip out of the corner, but Planter was now the stronger and surer. Across the room he followed his enemy, playing ever for the body—kidneys, abdomen, heart. Disbro was hanging on, his breath came in choking grunts. Planter struggled loose, and sank one clean, hard right uppercut.

Disbro spun off of his feet, fell across the overturned table, and lay moaning and gasping.

"Had enough?" Planter challenged.

Disbro was crawling on the floor, trying to grab the pistol. Planter sprang in, stamped on Disbro's knuckles. Disbro had only the strength and breath for one scream, and collapsed.

Abruptly Skygors entered, Skygors with hard eyes and leveled weapons. "What," demanded one, "is this?"

Disbro, helped to his shaky feet, pointed to Planter. "He—he—refused," he managed to wheeze out.

Disbro nodded, and Planter felt a sudden rush of joy. They would drive him forth, as they used to drive forth unprofitable female slaves. And he would find the Nest again, and Mara.

He was being herded along a passage, up stairs. The Skygors who guarded him kept their weapons close against his ribs. "No escape," they promised him balefully.

He wondered at that, but only a little. Now they had brought him out upon an open, railed bridge between two buildings. Below was water, above the thick Venusian mist. "Jump," a Skygor bade him.

"I need no second chance," Planter replied, breezily, and dived in.

He still wore the scanty costume of a slave, and it allowed him to strike out easily for the edge of the pool. Behind him the Skygors were discussing him, but in their own guttural tongue which he could not understand. As he swam, he studied the city beneath the water.

He meant to come back and assail that city some time, and there must be worthwhile secrets to note. For instance, he was now aware that this pool was artificial—he made out the sluices and gates of a large dam. To one side was a spacious submarine chamber that must be the clockwork-jammed cellar where his erstwhile companions, the slaves, worked.

But something else was under water, something that moved darkly, but had arms and legs, though it was as vast as an elephant. It was approaching him swiftly, knowingly.

Now he knew why he had been told, with such a voice of doom, to jump into the water.

*

Planter's blood was still up because of that brisk battle with Disbro. He was young, strong, in gilt-edge condition. His new impulse was to keep on fighting, against the thing which had the size, the intention, and apparently the appetite, to engulf him.

The huge swimmer was a Skygor, of tremendous size. Logic in the back of Planter's head bade him not to be amazed; on this damp, fecund world, monsters of such sort were not too unthinkable. As it broke surface, he heard a hubbub like many steam sirens. The smaller Skygors, on housetops and bridges, were all chanting some sort of ear-bursting litany, waving their flippers in unison. Plainly they worshiped this giant of their race. He, Planter, was a gift—a sacrifice.

He swam speedily, but his pursuer was speedier still. With ponderous overhand strokes it overhauled him. An arm as long as his body, with a flipper-hand like a tremendous scoop shovel, extended to clutch at him. A mouth like an open trunk gaped, large enough to gulp him bodily.

Only one thing to do. He did it—dived at once, turning under water and darting below and in an opposite direction from the great swimmer. By pure, happy chance, his kicking feet struck the soft cushion of its mighty belly, and he heard the thrumming gasp of the wind he knocked out of it. Coming up beyond, he swam desperately toward a nearby building. If he could climb up, away, from this huge, hungry being.

"No, not here!" That was a Skygor, poking its ugly smirking face from a window-hole. He tried to seize the sill to draw himself out of the water, and it lifted a dagger to slash at his knuckles.

But then it gasped, wriggled. The paw opened, the knife fell. Planter managed to catch it as it struck the water. A moment later he saw what had happened—big human hands were fastened on the slimy throat from behind. The Skygor, struggling, was pulled back out of sight. In its place showed the flat, simple features of Max.

"Huhh!" gurgled Max. "You in trouble, Mr. Planter?"

He put out a hand to help. At the same moment a monstrous flipper struck at Planter, driving him deep under water.

He filled his lungs with air at the last moment, spun and tried to kick away. His enemy had its hooked claws in his clothing and was drawing him toward the dark cavern of its mouth. Planter struck with the knife he had snatched, and buried the blade in the slimy-green lower lip of the creature. It let go, and a cloud of blood—red as the blood of Earth's creatures—suddenly obscured the water, so that Planter could attempt another escape.

He reached the top once again. The giant held itself half out of the water, big and grotesque as some barbaric sculpture, one webbed hand held against its wounded mouth. As Planter came into view, its big, bitter eyes caught sight of him. Dropping its hand, it howled at him. All the Skygors at their watch-points echoed that howl and began to repeat their uncouth litany once again. The monster pursued as before.

But from his watch-window, Max threw his burly pugilist's body.

Coarsely built Max might have been. Stupid he undoubtedly was. Cowardly and clumsy he was not. As he flung himself into space, he shifted so that his feet were down. He drove them hard between the shoulders of the huge Skygor demon, and the impact of his flying weight drove it under water.

"Get out of here!" yelled Max at Planter. "Get out!"

He had time for no more, for he, too, submerged. Planter clasped his knife in his teeth, and turned in the water. He could not desert that plucky rescuer.

*

Righting itself, the big Skygor grimaced under the troubled, gory surface. It was having trouble—more trouble than ever before in its freakish, idle, overstuffed life as deity and champion of the community. Two alien dwarfs, of a species it had looked on hitherto as only enticing meat, were viciously attacking and wounding it. Hunger was overlaid by a stern lust for vengeance.

It spied one of the enemy very close, swimming away. Max was not as much at home in the water as Planter, and he could not dodge its grasping talons. Treading water, the thing hoisted him clear, as a child might lift a kitten. Its other paw struck him, with openwebbed palm, hard as a mule's kick.

Max went limp. Once again that awful mouth opened to its full extent.

"No, you don't!" cried Planter, battling his way close. For a second time he drove with the knife, sheathing it to the hilt in a slate-colored chest, close to one armpit.

A fountain of blood sprang forth, drenching his face and weapon hand. He dragged strongly downward, felt his weapon point grating on bone, then coming free. That was a terrible wound, but not a disabling one. In a frenzy of pain and rage, the Skygor giant threw Max far away into the water, and

44

whirled to look for its other tormentor.

But Planter had dived yet again. The fresh blood obscured his passage as before. He came up, panted for air, and seized the limp wrist of Max. As he kicked away for shore, he heard the whine and *splat* of a missile.

The Skygors were shooting at him.

He bobbed under, bringing Max with him. As he fought through the water, he felt his friend quiver and beat with his hands. He felt fierce joy. Max was alive, he too, would escape. He had to come up.

"Duck down, Planter," Max told him at once. "They're going to give us another volley."

His voice was suddenly intelligent, his words sensible and articulate. Planter took the advice, swam forward again.

"Shore's that way," said Max, when they came up. "Can you make it? Give me your hand."

The ex-pugilist was climbing over a tangle of roots, to solid ground at last. Planter made shift to follow him.

"What—happened—" Planter barely whispered.

Max laughed, very cheerfully. "What a wallop that sea-elephant has! I guess it knocked my senses back into me. Another belt dizzied me back on Earth. So it's logical that—"

Yes, logical.... Max was no longer a dim, stupid child in a big man's body.

Planter felt himself weakening. He had fought himself out. Even as he turned toward the jungle, he stumbled and fell, rolled over on his back.

He could see the whole surface of the water-city. Skygors were coming in throngs to recapture him, crowded aboard their inflated boats, or swimming. For ahead of them, something like an awful goblin was scrambling out—the mighty freak he and Max had dodged up to now. It stood erect on powerful, awkward legs, its eyes probing here and there to pick up the trail of its prey.

Planter tried to tell Max to run, but his strength and breath were spent. He could only lie and watch. Max had torn up a kind of sapling, whirled it aloft like a club. The tottering colossus approached them, heavily and grimly. It grinned relentlessly, its bloody muzzle opened and slavered.

Out of the jungle moved another figure. A smaller Skygor? No—*Mara!*

She sprang across the prostrate form of Planter. He managed to rise to an elbow, just as she planted herself in the way of the oncoming destruction. It loomed high above her, paws lifted to seize and crush her. But she had lifted her crossbow.

Pale fire flashed. The string hummed. At a scant five feet of distance she slammed a pen-missile full into the thing's immense chest.

It staggered back from her, its face gone into a terrible oversize mask of awful pain. Those great legs, like dark, gnarled stumps, bowed and bent. It fell uncouthly, supported itself on spread hands. Planter could see the hole Mara had burned in it, a great red raw pit the size of a bushel basket. Then it was down, motionless. Dead.

Max had helped Planter up. "Can you run?" he was demanding.

"No! No!" Mara interposed, hurrying back to them. "Not run! Fight!"

"Fight?" Planter echoed, rather idiotically.

"Fight the Skygors! See, your friends have come!"

Through the jungle to the water's edge pressed other human figures, in Terrestrial overalls and helmets.

*

A slim, square-faced man in the neatest of overall costumes had grabbed Planter's elbow. It was beginning to rain again. Thunder sounded, like Skygors grumbling high in the mist. "Quick!" said the square-faced man. "You're Planter, aren't you? And that other man—but where's Disbro."

Planter pointed toward the water-city. "Who are you?" he demanded, as if they had all day.

"Dr. Hommerson. Commanding this new expedition. Ten of us in the big new ship started when they reported you landing safely. We cracked up, not far from where your ship bogged down. This girl found us, said—"

"Whatever she said was true!" cut in Planter. "Quick, defend yourself against those Skygors."

"They'll defend themselves against us," rejoined Dr. Hommerson bleakly. "If they're smart, and if they're lucky."

46

His companions had formed a sort of skirmish line among the thickest stems at the water's edge. With a variety of weapons—force-rifles, machine guns, one or two portable grenade throwers—they had opened on the Skygors.

The amphibian dwellers in the water-city had started to chase Planter and Max, but the destruction of their giant kinsman had daunted and immobilized them. Now they had something else to shake their courage, which was never too great. Well-aimed shots were picking them off, in the boats, in the water, on the housetops and bridges.

"Don't show yourselves more than is necessary!" Dr. Hommerson was barking. "If they know there's only a handful of us, they might—" He unlimbered a patent pistol, one with a long barrel, a magazine of fourteen rounds in the stock, and a wooden holster that could fit into a slot and form a makeshift butt like that of a rifle. Lifting this to his shoulder, he began to shoot at such of the Skygors as still showed themselves.

Mara had rushed to Planter's side. "They're retreating!" she cried. "The spell—remember the *spell!*"

True enough, he'd forgotten. That wild, unmanning storm of noise that defended Skygor country, that had knocked him into their webbed fingers as a captive and slave, might begin at any moment. Even now the Skygors were retiring inside their buildings, but with a certain purposeful orderliness. As Planter watched, Max ran up to his other side.

"She's telling the truth. I know all about that thing they sound off," he said breathlessly in his new, knowing voice. "When I was with Disbro—working for him—I had a look at it."

"Stop your ears," Mara was bidding. "Quick! A rag from your garment will do!"

She ripped away part of Planter's shirt, tore the piece in two, and thrust wads into his ears with her forefinger. Max was plugging his own ears. Then the sound began.

When it began, nobody could say. Suddenly, it was there, filling space with itself as though it were a crushing solid thing.

Planter, even with his ears partially muffled, almost collapsed. His body vibrated as before in every fiber, only not unendurably. He saw Max reel, but stay on his feet. Dr. Hommerson's men, a moment ago almost in the victor's position, were down, floundering in half-crazy agony. Planter understood, in that rear compartment of his mind that was always diagnosing strange things, even in the moment of worst danger.

The Skygors were ill-cultured, poor of spirit, prospered chiefly by ideas stolen from the human beings they enslaved. But they understood sound waves, could use them roughly as an electrician might use electric vibrations. There were all the tales he had heard, of a chord on the organ that shattered window panes, of certain orators who could employ voice-frequencies to spellbind and impassion their audiences. This was something like that, only more so.

Then he saw that Mara, who had thought of saving his ears, was down at his feet.

"Mara!" he cried, though nobody could have heard him. He knelt, ripping away more rags of his shirt. He crammed them furiously into her ears. She stirred, got to her knees. She, too, could endure it now, and she smiled at him, drawnly.

"I knew you would come back," her lips formed words. "David Planter—my David Planter—"

Then she was up, crossbow at the ready.

Because back came the Skygors, a wave of them in boats and as swimmers. Sure of their victory through sound, they were going to mop up the attackers.

Max had a rifle. He lifted it, but on inspiration Planter leaped at him and gestured for him to hold fire. From beside one of the fallen Terrestrials he caught a grenade thrower. It was a simple amplification of an ordinary rifle. Upon the muzzle fitted a metal device like a bottomless bottle, the neck clamping tight to the barrel. Into the spread body of the bottle could be slid a cylindrical grenade, the size and shape of a condensed-milk tin. The grenade was pierced with a hole, and the gun, if fired, would send its bullet through that hole, while the gases of the exploding powder operated to hurl the grenade far and forcefully and accurately.

*

Planter had never used one, but he had seen them used. A quick check showed him that the rifle's magazine was full. From the belt of the fallen man he twitched a grenade, slipped it into place. He knelt, placed the rifle butt on the soggy mass of rotting vegetation that made up the shoreside jungle floor. By guess, he slanted his weapon about forty-five degrees forward. The foremost press of Skygors approached.

Bang! At Planter's trigger-touch, the grenade rose upward. For a moment the three conscious watchers could see it, outlined against the upper mists at the hesitating apex of its flight. Then it fell, too far to demoralize the first ranks of Skygors, but smashing two inflated boats in its explosion and tossing several slimy-green forms like chips through the air. Planter slid in another grenade, worked the rifle-bolt, and raised the weapon to his shoulder.

It spoke again, louder even than the din of the noisemaker Mara called the "spell." This time it struck water among the leading Skygors, and exploded on contact. Three or four sank abruptly, several more thrashed the water into pinky-red foam in the pain of bad wounds, the rest wavered.

Now Max opened fire with his rifle, and Mara with her crossbow. Both scored hits, and the Skygors gave back. Something was going wrong, they were realizing. The destroying sound was not paralyzing their enemy. Meanwhile, it was best to take cover. Some ducked under the water, others fell back toward the buildings.

"Dynamite 'em!" cried Planter, forgetting that he could not be heard. Stooping, he stripped away the whole beltful of grenades from its helpless owner. He whirled it around his head as though he were throwing a hammer on an athletic field, and sent it flying out over the water. The shock of its fall into the depths set it off—all grenades at once. Skygors came bounding to the top, twitching feebly. The explosion had destroyed them, as fish are destroyed by the shock of detonating dynamite in nearby waters.

Then the paralyzing noise stopped.

Hommerson was the first man up. He was dazed and groggy, but fight was the first impulse that woke in him. Mara, Max and Planter dragged others to

49

their feet, shook and shouted their senses back into them.

"They're retreating!" Planter yelled. "Let's counter-attack!"

Close in to shore drifted one of the abandoned boats. Max had run into the water, dragging it closer. The Terrestrials tumbled aboard, and one of them got the paddle-wheel running. Planter, at the bow directing fire at any Skygors who showed their heads, saw that Mara had not come along. He worried a moment, then worried no more. She was shouting in the jungle, and other voices—feminine voices—answered her. More of the crossbow-girls were coming to help.

The boat made a landing at the building where Planter had first been dragged to slavery. It was not made for defense, and the invaders split into small parties, ranging the corridors and outer bridges. Planter, hurrying downstairs, heard the *spat* of the Skygor pen-missiles, with the replying crackle of gunfire. After a while, Mara and other girls began to shout and chatter. They had also found a boat and had come over.

On the floor, above the basement where the slaves worked, he came face to face with a Skygor, who lifted his arms appealingly, in the surrender gesture that must be universal among all creatures who have arms. "I want no fight," begged this one. "You are master."

"Then come downstairs," snapped Planter. He clattered down, among the slaves. "Stop work!" he bawled, almost as loudly as a Skygor, and the men, bred to obey big voices, did so.

"Outside!" was Planter's next command. One or two moved to obey, others hung back.

"Outside," the surrendered Skygor echoed Planter, and they came obediently. Planter hurried them to their quarters, then slammed the door to the big workshop.

"That closes down your power plants," he commented to the Skygor. "Now, quick! Which way to the controls of the dam?"

"Dam?" the Skygor repeated stupidly.

Planter caught the green shoulders and shook the creature roughly. It was larger than he, but cowered. "I will show," it yielded, and led him away. In a nearby corridor were huge handles, three of them, like pivoted clinker-bars. Planter seized one, pulled it down. He heard waters roaring. He pulled another.

"You will drain the pool," protested the Skygor.

"I want to drain the pool," Planter said.

"Then—" The Skygor caught the third lever and pulled it down.

Planter hurried upstairs again. His prisoner kept at his heels.

"Why did you help me?" he asked it.

"Because you conquer," was the booming reply. "The conquered must obey."

"I think you believe that stuff, like the slaves," Planter sniffed.

"Of course, I believe," responded the Skygor.

From the upper levels came Hommerson's voice:

"Planter! These frog-folk are giving up! They haven't any fight left in them!"

But Planter paused, on a landing. He looked into a small office, where two human figures stood close together.

One was Max. The other was Disbro. Max had Disbro by the throat, not shaking or wrestling him. Only squeezing.

"Max!" called Planter. "Why—"

"Why not?" countered Max plausibly. "Planter, I think maybe you were the thick-headed one. You always tried to get along with Disbro, as if he was honest. I was a crazy-house case, but from the first I knew he was wrong. It took the return of sense to understand that the only thing to do was this."

He let go, and Disbro fell on the floor like an empty suit of clothes.

Max brushed his hands together, as if to clear them of dust.

"I wonder how long I've wanted to do that," he said. "Let's go up and watch the final mop-up."

*

Out of the mud pool where once a snake-armed krau had pursued Planter, the combined strength of many arms was hoisting the bogged ship. Cables had been woven through pulley-blocks at the tops of the biggest and strongest poolside stems. Free men of Venus, once slaves, hauled on these cables in brief, concerted rhythms. Here and there in the rope-gangs toiled a Skygor, accepting defeat and companionship with the same mild grace. Women—free women—laughed and encouraged, and now and again threw themselves into the tugging labor that was a game, Max oversaw everything.

Near by, machete had hewn a little clearing. Here a waterproof tent over a beehive framework sheltered Planter and Dr. Hommerson. They watched as the ship, its bow-rockets toiling to help the tugging cables, finally stirred out of its bed.

Hommerson smiled. "Time to hold a sort of recapitulation, isn't it? As in old-fashioned mystery yarns, when the case is solved and the danger done away with? Of course, it all happened suddenly, but we can say this much:

"The Skygor mistake was that of every softened master setup. They had a half-rigged defense against mild dangers, and never looked for real trouble. They beat that Seventeenth Century space-expedition simply because Terrestrials of that day hadn't the proper weapons. Otherwise, man might have been ruling here for four hundred years and more."

"The Skygors did have one tremendous device," observed Planter. "That super-siren that deadens you by sound waves."

Hommerson laughed. "And which providentially did what all clockwork mechanisms are apt to do—ran down. It's dismantled now, anyway. We're a fuel-engine civilization, and the Skygors will have to wonder and admire a while before they steal our new tricks."

Planter fingered another trophy of the battle, a great brass-bound log book, old and yellowed, but still readable. "This answers more riddles," he put in. "The record of those ancient fugitives from Cromwell. Who'd have thought that their times could produce a successful flight from planet to planet?"

"It was a great century," reminded Hommerson. "Don't forget that they also invented the microscope, the balloon, the principle of maneuverable armies. Their century began with Francis Bacon and ended with Sir Isaac Newton. That rocket fuel, which the Skygors only half understood and used for ammunition—"

"Doctor!" broke in Planter. "Do you remember the old Puritan tales of witches, flying on what seemed like broomsticks?"

"And Cyrano de Bergerac, in France about 1640, writing a tale of a rocket to the moon? We simply forgot that they had something then. The real complete knowledge flew here to Venus, and waited for our age to develop it again from the beginning."

It was so. Planter pondered awhile, and while he pondered one of the expedition came in to make a report.

"We can send back three in this ship when it's set," he said to Hommerson. "Who are you taking, sir?"

"These two who survived the earlier flight, Planter and his big, tough friend. The rest of you can wait and develop a landing field."

Planter spoke: "Did you see the girl called Mara out there?"

"She was watching us," said the man. "Finally she went into the jungle."

"With no message for me?"

"No message for anybody."

"Dr. Hommerson," said Planter, "pick someone else instead of me. Here I stay."

Hommerson looked up sharply. "Until the next ship comes?"

"Here I stay," repeated Planter. "From now on."

He sought a certain jungle trail, one he had traversed before. "Mara!" he called down it.

She was not hard to catch up with, for she was not walking fast. As he came alongside, she looked at him with eyes too bright to be dry.

"You came to bid goodbye," she suggested.

He shook his head. The mist seemed less than ever before on Venus. "No. Never goodbye."

"Isn't the ship leaving?"

"Leaving, all right. But not with me in it. This is home now."

She looked down at her sandalled feet, and one hand played with the dagger in her belt. "Methought you would be glad to regain Earth."

"Earth? Other people gained it long ago." He pulled her hand away from the dagger-hilt. "Stop fiddling with that stabbing-iron, there's no fighting to be done just now.

"You said I was yours," he told her furiously. "You said it just as if you'd won me in a game of some sort."

"And you brushed it aside without answering me. You had none of it."

"Hang it, Mara, a man decides those things! And I've been deciding them. You're the bravest creature I ever knew—the most graceful—the most honest. You did love me once. Have you stopped?"

"I have not stopped," she said. "But why have you waited to say these words?"

"I haven't had time, and I'm going to have little time for a while, what with organization and building and food-hunting and colonizing. But—"

Her mouth, close at hand, was too delectable. He kissed her fiercely. She jumped away, startled, then uttered a little breathless laugh.

"That likes me well," she told him. "Let us do it again."